BEWARE!!
DO NOT READ THIS
BOOK FROM
BEGINNING TO END!

Yes! Mom and Dad are out of town, and your sweet old grandma is coming to take care of you. You are ready for freedom. But are you ready for . . . *Grandma*?

The terror starts at the train station, with two old ladies who *both* look exactly like your grandma.

If you go after the Grandma who is still on the train, you might end up battling aliens with eyes the size of ping-pong balls. Or jumping from a hovering helicopter! If you go home with the other Grandma, we have one piece of advice for you:

Stay out of the rose garden!

This scary adventure is all about you. You decide what will happen. And you decide how terrifying the scares will be!

Start on *PAGE 1*. Then follow the instructions at the bottom of each page. *You* make the choices. If you choose well, you'll survive this adventure. But if you make the wrong choice . . . BEWARE!

SO TAKE A DEEP BREATH. CROSS YOUR FINGERS. AND TURN TO PAGE 1 TO *GIVE YOURSELF GOOSEBUMPS!*

READER BEWARE —
YOU CHOOSE THE SCARE!

Look for more
GIVE YOURSELF GOOSEBUMPS adventures
from R.L. STINE

R.L. STINE
GIVE YOURSELF
Goosebumps®

SECRET AGENT
GRANDMA

AN
APPLE
PAPERBACK

SCHOLASTIC INC.
New York Toronto London Auckland
Sydney New Delhi Hong Kong

A PARACHUTE PRESS BOOK

No part of this publication may be reproduced, in whole or in part, or stored in a retrieval system, or transmitted in any form or by any means, electronic, mechanical, photocopying, recording, or otherwise, without written permission of the publisher. For information regarding permission, write to: Scholastic Inc., 557 Broadway, New York, NY 10012.

ISBN-13: 978-0-590-84775-9

This edition is for sale in Indian subcontinent only.

First Scholastic Printing, April 1997
Reprinted by Scholastic India Pvt. Ltd., March 2008
January; August 2010; November 2011; January 2012;
July; December 2013; August; December 2014;
August; November 2015

Printed at Shivam Offset Press, New Delhi

"Nothing is going to happen to me," you shout down to your mother.

She gazes up at you from the bottom of the stairs. Her packed suitcases sit waiting by the front door. You recognize that worried look on her face.

"Do you remember everything I told you?" she asks. Her forehead wrinkles in concern. "Or should I write it down?"

"Mom! I'm not a baby." You plop onto the top step of the staircase and repeat your instructions for the fifth time. "I take a cab to the railroad station. I wait on the platform on the incoming side of the station. Grandma's train arrives at one P.M. I'll know her by the yellow stretch pants and purple shirt she'll be wearing. Then, if she hasn't been arrested by the fashion police for wearing such a wacko outfit —"

"Don't make fun of your grandmother," your mother cuts in. "She's unusual, but I'm sure you two will get along fine."

"Your mother's right," your dad adds, coming through the front door. "Your grandma is full of surprises."

Yeah sure, you think. How is some little old lady going to surprise me?

Go on to PAGE 2

2

Your dad picks up the remaining suitcases and heads back out to the car. Your mother doesn't move. You flash her your most trustworthy smile.

She sighs. "I guess you'll be all right," she says uncertainly.

"Of course I will!" you assure her. "What could happen?"

You follow your mom out to the car and wave as your parents drive away. The moment their car turns the corner you leap into the air. "Freedom!" you cry.

No parents for a whole week! Just a seventy-five-year-old grandma. She'll probably spend the whole time snoozing on the sun porch. You'll practically be on your own!

The cab arrives and you hop in. You instruct the driver to take you to the train station.

But as he nears the station you have a pang of doubt. You haven't seen your grandmother since you were a little kid. You wonder if you'll recognize her.

Worry until PAGE 3.

You may not recognize Grandma's face, you tell yourself, but you'll definitely spot her purple-and-yellow outfit. Besides, she'll know *you* from the photos your parents sent her.

You pay the driver and hop out.

Hey! That's weird, you think. Why was your name announced over the loudspeaker? You rush to the information booth inside the station, wondering what could be wrong.

"You just paged me," you tell the young man in the booth.

"You've got a call." He hands you a phone.

"Hello?" There's a lot of static on the line. You can barely hear, but it's definitely your mom's voice.

"We're — psst — on the plane . . . pfffft — home immediately!"

"What? I can't hear you!" you shout into the phone. "Do you want me to go home? What about Grandma?"

"Pssssfffft — danger . . . grandmother . . . "

That's all you hear. Then the line goes dead.

Turn to PAGE 108.

4

You're surprised to see your friends Chuck and Ginny rushing toward you.

"Hey, guys," you greet them. "I'm here to meet my grandmother. How about you?"

"We're going to the hockey game, remember?" Chuck tells you. "I invited you."

You remember. You couldn't go because of Grandma's arrival.

"Our moms are letting us take the train on our own!" Ginny adds. "Of course, we had to promise to stay out of trouble." Ginny giggles. "As if!"

"Have fun with Grandma," Chuck teases. They board the train.

You sigh jealously as you scan the thinning crowd.

Still no grandmother.

Is this what your mother had been trying to tell you? That your grandmother wasn't coming after all?

You're about to leave the station when you hear something that stops you in your tracks. Something terrible.

What makes your blood run cold? Find out on PAGE 86.

Wait and see seems like the best thing to do.

But you don't want to do it here!

You double-check the newspaper article. "Let's get back here when the meteor shower is supposed to begin," you instruct Sophie and Andrew. "Then maybe we'll find out how it all ties in together."

You leave a note for Grandma and head over to the park to play Frisbee. You can't help wondering what will happen. You're so distracted you miss the Frisbee every single time.

At seven P.M. sharp, you, Sophie, and Andrew creep back to the rose garden. It looks spooky in the dark. The roses seem even larger than they did before.

There's no sign of Grandma.

Turn to PAGE 15.

6

CRRRRCKKK! you hear again.

You peer up into the tree by your front gate. "There's a man up there!" you exclaim.

"Don't look up!" the man in the tree orders.

You, Sophie, and Andrew immediately stare down at the ground.

"Tell me," the man continues, "is your grandma around?"

Your head snaps up. "Do you want to see her?" you demand.

"No! No!" the man tells you in a hoarse whisper. "I want to make sure she *doesn't* see me!"

"She's in the back," you tell him.

The man leaps down out of the tree. His brown eyes narrow as he studies your face. He seems to be sizing you up.

Two can play at that game, you figure. You check him out. His black hair is cut very short. He wears torn black jeans and a black T-shirt.

"So who are you?" Sophie blurts.

"Special Agent Bendrey," the man says. "I'm an alien investigator. And I think the four of us should have a chat."

Should you trust this guy? Maybe he can help you.

Or maybe he's another impostor!

Get rid of Bendrey on PAGE 19.
Spill the beans on PAGE 27.

"Forget it," you scold the cab driver. "That's snooping."

The front door pops open.

"What's taking you so long?" Grandma demands. She strides to the cab, grasps the suitcase handles, and lifts both bags.

"I need to start working out," the cab driver mutters.

"Come on, Cookie!" Grandma beams at you. "Show me my room."

"It's at the top of the stairs," you tell her.

You follow her into the house.

"Perfect," she croons, entering the guest room. "Right over the rose garden. I'll watch my babies growing out of the ground."

Did you hear right? "Your babies?" you repeat.

Grandma spins around and stares at you. Then she smiles. "I think of the rose bushes as my babies," she explains.

Grandma isn't just unusual, you think. She's plain weird!

You peer down. You've never paid much attention to the garden before. It takes up most of the backyard. Dozens of flowers sprout from each bush. Okay, so this year they're wacky colors. And they *are* much larger than usual.

But basically, what's the big deal?

Grandma suddenly stiffens beside you!

Find out what's wrong on PAGE 30.

The three new Grandmas chatter at once. "So there you are!"

"Hope number three didn't cause trouble!"

"Is everyone all right in here?"

"What's going on?" you scream.

Silence fills the train car.

All of the Grandmas stare at you. So do Chuck and Ginny.

"Excuse me for yelling," you say. "But would someone please explain to me what's happening here?"

Grandma #1 laughs. "I was just getting to that!" she tells you. "Allow me to introduce my clones."

Then she explains the whole unbelievable story.

Your grandma is a top government scientist working on a secret cloning project. A project *everyone* seems to want to get their hands on! That's why she's coming to stay with you — to hide out.

You're the luckiest kid in the world. For the next month you have five Grandmas. And they all spoil you!

THE END

You gaze down at the garden, holding your breath.

"Nothing's moving," Sophie says.

"No sounds," Andrew adds hopefully.

You nod. Could you have done it? Did you actually destroy the aliens?

You open your mouth to say something. But then your jaw drops.

Dozens of wormy aliens slither out from under the mattress. And they're bigger than they were five minutes ago!

"It didn't work!" you wail.

"Maybe the mattress was too soft," Andrew says.

"It wasn't heavy enough," you realize. "Throw everything you can get your hands on!"

Frantically, you grab a chair and footstool. Out the window! Andrew and Sophie toss down Grandma's suitcases. You hurl out the stereo and a radio. They land with a crash. The radio blasts on.

There's nothing left to throw. And the aliens are still swarming around in the garden!

Turn to PAGE 130.

You don't have a moment to lose. The train car below you is filled with those creatures! And they've found you! They'll be climbing up after you any minute now!

"Geronimo!" you shout to Chuck and Ginny.

Then you leap off the train!

Oops! Bad timing. The train is going over a bridge. A very high bridge.

It's a loooooooong way down.

So long, in fact, that you have time to read the big banner hanging on the side of the train car.

Evanstown High School Annual Costume Party.

Too bad you didn't notice it sooner.

Say good-bye, party animal!

THE END

"Out! Now!" Grandma rasps.

She heard you.

You and your friends crawl out from under the bed.

You gaze at the horrifying creature in front of you. Grandma's human face is shoved up on top of her head, as if it were a Halloween mask. In its place is an oozing blob of flesh. A single yellow eye gleams in the center.

"Interfering fools!" the Grandma-creature booms. "Now I will have to destroy you ahead of schedule!"

Before you can protest, the creature spits at you.

Gross! A long, sticky strand of saliva flies out of her mouth. It attaches to your forehead and wraps around Sophie's and Andrew's heads. It burns where it touches your skin.

"Yuck!" Sophie shrieks.

The creature spits over and over again. The strands are like a spider's web. Soon, you and your friends are completely encased in a sticky cocoon. You can't see a thing.

"You can't escape the pod," the creature informs you. "And the acid in the web will eat through your flesh."

You hear her leave the room.

This is one sticky situation you can't get out of. So this must be

THE END.

The station rattles and shakes around you. Your hands clutch the information counter so tightly your fingers cramp. A framed picture on the wall behind the clerk crashes to the floor.

Get me out of here!

You spin and dash out of the station. Your heart pounds and your breath comes in gasps as you race along the sidewalk.

Whoops! Too bad you weren't looking where you were going. Otherwise you would have seen the garbage truck *before* you landed in the middle of the gunk, the goo, and the gross slime.

Eeeewwwww. Hold your nose and close the book quickly! You stink! You've come to a very smelly

END!

"We'll throw stuff at them." You point to Grandma's window. "From up there."

The aliens are busy eating and don't notice you sneaking into the house. You race to Grandma's room. "They're all crowded together in that corner," you cry, glancing out the window. "Even Grandma. We might be able to get them all at once!"

"Let's use this!" Andrew struggles to get the mattress off the bed. You and Sophie help him drag it to the window.

"One! Two!" You strain to lift the mattress over the sill. "Three!"

The mattress drops directly on top of the group of aliens.

Did it work? Find out on PAGE 9.

You know what the letters spell! It's so simple that you laugh at yourself for not getting it sooner.

EMPLEH. Whoever wrote the message on the inside of the window didn't realize it would be read backward on the outside. EMPLEH is HELP ME, written backwards. You say it out loud.

"What did you say, dear?" Grandma asks. "Do you need help with something?"

You are about to tell her about the message when something you see inside the train stops you. You stare past the letters on the window and into the compartment.

Your eyes widen. You blink several times. You take a step closer to the window. Your nose presses up against the glass.

You don't believe what you're seeing!

What has you glued to the train window? Find out on PAGE 98.

"I bet nothing will happen," you say. "I'm sure there's a logical explanation for everything."

Before Sophie and Andrew can answer, the ground beneath your feet begins to rumble.

"What's going on?" Sophie cries.

You glance up. Dozens of meteors shoot across the sky. They light up the night. You can see the garden clearly.

And Grandma!

She stands in the middle of the roses. By the light of the meteor shower, you watch Grandma reach up and *pull off her face*!

You hear Sophie and Andrew gasp beside you. But you can't tear your eyes away. Grandma's new face oozes and bubbles. A single yellow eye blinks in the center of her forehead. Her thick purple tail thrashes wildly.

Surrounding her are dozens of purple pulsating eggs. The vibrations from the eggs make the ground shake.

Grandma lets out a bone-chilling howl.

Immediately, all the eggs burst open!

Turn to PAGE 43.

"Grandma!" you call again louder. "The roses!"

Grandma dashes toward you. She spots the hose and yanks it out of the bush. It gushes water.

"We have to turn it off in the garage," you tell her. "And I don't think I'm strong enough."

Grandma eyes you suspiciously. "Hmm," she murmurs.

But she heads for the garage.

You follow right behind her, with your fingers crossed.

Grandma enters the dark garage. You hold your breath.

"Eeeeyah!" Sophie shrieks and leaps down from a stack of cartons. She lands right on top of Grandma.

Andrew hurls himself onto the struggling pair. Sophie squeezes out from under Grandma and Andrew. Andrew wraps Grandma in your badminton net as they roll over and over.

You rush over. You and Sophie hold Grandma as Andrew wiggles out of the net.

Grandma stops struggling. "You never would have gotten away with this if it weren't for this dinky human disguise!" she snarls. "You humans are so weak."

You drape your bicycle chain around her and snap the lock shut. "But we got the best of you!" you retort.

Turn to PAGE 36.

"We'll keep an eye on the eggs for you," you tell Special Agent Bendrey.

He gives a sharp nod. "Good. You should be safe if you act like you believe that woman is your real grandma," he assures you. Then he takes off down the street.

"Wait!" you call after him. He never told you what you're supposed to do if the eggs hatch! But he's gone.

You, Sophie, and Andrew spend the rest of the afternoon up in your room. You take turns peering down at the garden.

"Still nothing," Sophie grumbles. "This is boring."

"Maybe it all ties in with the meteor shower tonight," you suggest. "We'll go downstairs right before it begins."

Later that evening, the three of you sneak out to the garden. Grandma is in the living room, watching TV.

You flick on your flashlights.

"Do we have our weapons?" you ask.

Sophie hands you three water guns. You fill them with bug spray. Hey, it's the best you can do on short notice.

"Okay," you announce. "We're ready."

Wait for the meteor shower to begin on PAGE 124.

18

You sigh. "The roses are great," you answer politely. "Mom says they're unusually large this year."

Grandma leans back in the car seat. "That is excellent."

"Why do you want to know about our garden?" you ask.

She pats your hand. "I lived in the house before your mother and father did. And I planted the eggs in the garden."

"Eggs?" you repeat. "How could you plant eggs?"

Grandma looks startled. "I meant seeds. I planted the seeds for the rose bushes."

"Those roses have been there as long as I can remember," you remark. "You must have planted them a long time ago."

"Fifteen years ago," Grandma tells you. "They're the only roses planted by the light of shooting stars." She chuckles. "Meteors, really. So many meteors fell, night turned into day."

The taxi pulls into your driveway.

"I must see the roses right away!" Grandma leaps out of the cab and disappears around the back of the house.

You stare after her. Was she always this weird?

The driver pops open the trunk to get Grandma's bags. He reaches in and tugs. And yanks. And grunts. And pulls.

Give the guy a hand on PAGE 101.

"Alien investigator? Great joke!" You force a laugh. "Isn't that funny, guys?" You turn to Sophie and Andrew, hoping they get what you're doing.

"Total laugh riot!" Sophie guffaws.

"Had me in stitches," Andrew adds.

"Listen," you say to Bendrey. "We have an appointment. We don't have time for games." You march briskly down the walk.

"You'll be sorry," Bendrey calls after you. "You could really use my help!"

You ignore him. You hurry down the street, Sophie and Andrew on your heels.

"Are you sure . . . ?" Andrew begins.

You glare at him and he shuts up.

Of course you're not sure! you think. But you didn't trust that special agent guy.

You just hope you don't regret refusing to speak to him.

Turn to PAGE 25.

"I want to help find my real grandma!" you declare.

"Good choice, kid." Bendrey smiles at you. "Come on!"

He leads you through town. In a few minutes, you, Sophie, Andrew, and Special Agent Bendrey stand outside an abandoned rail yard. One train car sits alone in the back of the yard.

"The aliens dragged your grandma into the last train car," Bendrey explains. "Then they unhooked the car from the one in front of it and brought it here."

You gaze at the nearly empty train yard. You shiver. Just being here gives you the creeps. Knowing aliens are inside that train car make your knees wobble with fear.

"Let's go!" Bendrey leads you, Sophie, and Andrew to a small opening in the fence. You crawl through and sneak toward the train car. The sun is setting, throwing weird shadows. Your heart pounds so hard, you're afraid the aliens inside might hear it!

Suddenly, the night sky brightens.

"The meteor shower!" Sophie gasps.

"Oh, no!" Bendrey exclaims.

Why is he upset about the meteor shower? you wonder.

Turn to PAGE 42.

"Ticket?" you repeat. You smile up at the conductor.

He doesn't smile back.

You spot Chuck and Ginny entering the compartment. Great!

"Hi! I was looking for you!" You dart past the conductor and join your friends. "He wants to see my ticket," you explain. You hope they'll come up with an idea. Or some cash.

"If you weren't always late, you would have your ticket!" Ginny scolds. Then she winks at you.

"That's right," Chuck tells the conductor. "My mom is picking us up in Evanstown. She'll pay when we arrive."

"We promised our parents we wouldn't get into trouble," Ginny gushes.

You want to gag. But Ginny's act works.

"Okay." The conductor pats Ginny's head. "As long as the ticket gets paid for." He strolls out of the train car.

"What was that about?" Chuck demands. "Why are you on the train? Aren't you supposed to be with your grandmother?"

You tell them about the strange scene you witnessed.

"That woman might be my real grandma!" you exclaim. "You have to help me search the train!"

Ginny and Chuck gaze at each other. "No way . . . " Chuck begins.

Your heart sinks all the way to PAGE 59.

You don't know what to do next. So you sit at the kitchen table and scarf down a few brownies. Then you glance out the window — and notice someone sneaking around your garage!

"Come on!" you shout. You dash out the door. Andrew and Sophie follow on your heels. But you're too late. The guy has already disappeared into the garage.

You charge through the door. And gasp.

Grandma has transformed!

She's covered in green scales and has sprouted seven arms and three heads. All three heads are smiling into the intruder's video camera.

"What's going on?" you demand.

"I'm interviewing your grandma," the guy explains. "She'll be a great story!"

"Cookie!" Grandma scolds. "You're in the way. You'll block my best angle."

Best angle? With three heads, there are plenty of angles to choose from!

Turn to PAGE 24.

You race to Grandma #2 in the doorway.

"Keep away from us!" you shout at the other Grandma. Chuck and Ginny rush to your side. "You're not my grandma!"

Anger, then worry, flashes across Grandma #1's face. "Wait! Don't —"

But you all charge out of the baggage car before she can say anything else.

You and Grandma #2 get out at the next station. Ginny and Chuck continue on to the hockey game.

"Grandma, you wouldn't believe what was going on in that train!" you tell her as you wait for the train back home. "There were alien creatures with yellow ping-pong eyes and . . ."

You hear a strange gurgling sound beside you. You glance over at Grandma.

No! It can't be!

Your stomach twists in fear and disgust. Grandma is peeling off her skin! A slimy mass of green pulsing flesh oozes underneath her Grandma face.

Boy, oh, boy. Did you pick the wrong Grandma!

THE END

24

"Your grandma was telling me all about her home planet," the reporter tells you.

"I'm so sorry I had to frighten you, dear," she tells you. "But I really needed the publicity. For my new movie."

Huh?

Seeing your confused look, all of Grandma's heads laugh. "Everyone knows you've got to come to Earth to get your big break!" she explains. "Lots of celebrities do it!"

"B-b-but —" you sputter. "What about the eggs in the rose garden? What about that fight we had when we captured you?"

"That's easy," Grandma scoffs. "The eggs were a dandy lunch. And the fight, well . . ." She shrugs. "I'm afraid I staged it. It was this young man's idea." She nods one head at the reporter. "He thought it would make a good lead-in. So, Cookie, what do you think of your grandma now?"

Your head swims. *My* grandma? Are you saying that I'm an alien like you?"

You feel faint just asking the question.

Grandma's answer is on PAGE 122. Well, what are you waiting for? Turn to the page!

Finally, you, Sophie, and Andrew arrive at the train station. The place is deserted. Your footsteps echo in the stillness as you trudge down the platform and into the station.

Even the information booth is closed.

"Now what?" Sophie asks.

"I'm thinking! I'm thinking!" you snap.

Andrew starts rubbing his head. Good. That means his brain is working. Maybe he'll figure out what to do.

You glance up and down the platform. A light in the distance begins getting larger. The platform begins to rumble.

Train coming in!

The train gives you an idea! You'll ask the conductor for a train schedule. Then maybe you can figure out where Grandma's train was headed. You explain your plan to Sophie and Andrew.

"Whatever." Sophie shrugs her shoulders. You can tell she doesn't think it's much of a plan.

The train roars into the station.

Now that's strange, you think. No one is getting on. And no one is getting off.

Turn to PAGE 39.

"It's so nice to see my Cookie!" Your grandmother gazes down at you. Her eyes sparkle. Two dimples crinkle her cheeks as she smiles.

You grin up at her. You must have imagined seeing that other woman. How could you have two grandmas? It's a dumb idea.

Get your grandma to a cab on PAGE 44.

Maybe this guy can help you, you reason. But you need to be careful. After all, you brought home the wrong Grandma!

"What do you mean — you're an alien investigator?" you ask.

The guy grins. "What does it sound like?"

"So why did you ask about Grandma?" Sophie demands.

Good question. You wish you had thought of it!

Special Agent Bendrey glances around. "Because I know that the woman claiming to be your grandmother is an impostor!"

Your mouth drops open. "How do you know?"

Bendrey's voice drops down to a low whisper. "Your real grandma is my partner!"

Turn to PAGE 48.

"We've got to wake Grandma," you tell the others. "We won't be able to escape any other way."

You, Ginny, and Chuck rush over to Grandma. You rub her hands and pat her face lightly. Finally, she comes around.

"My, my," she murmurs. "What am I doing up here?"

You describe everything that has happened. She clucks and shakes her head. "I was afraid they might be onto me."

Then Grandma tells you an amazing story.

She's a secret agent specializing in alien investigations!

"I've been tracking the evil Mithra-Dithra," she explains. "Obviously she assumed my identity. That's why you saw two of us at the train station. And why those creatures captured me."

Your head swims. This is unbelievable!

But you know your grandma is telling you the truth.

Grandma smiles at you. "You three did very well," she says. "I have an assignment for you. If you dare."

If you accept the assignment, turn to PAGE 34.
If you've had enough of aliens and danger, turn to PAGE 46.

"Let's see who's on the other side of the door," you tell Grandma.

She nods. "On my signal."

Grandma aims the device at the center of the door. You reach for the handle.

She nods again.

You take a deep breath and yank open the door.

"Aaaaaaaaah!" a boy shrieks, bursting into the bathroom.

Wham! The door smashes into your knee. The pain makes you weak.

The boy knocks into Grandma. The device flies from her hands — straight into the toilet. She falls against the wall.

"Get out! Get out! Get out!" the boy hollers.

You and Grandma are no match for him.

When you gotta go, you gotta go!

THE END

30

"There are two strangers at the back door," Grandma says. "Get rid of them. We don't need nosy neighbors poking around."

You glance out the window and smile.

"Those are just my friends, Sophie and Andrew," you assure her. "Hey, guys!" you call.

Sophie and Andrew look up. Sophie is the toughest kid you know. She's not afraid of anything. Bugs, snakes, rats — nothing scares her. You never, ever, dare her to do anything — because she'll do it and then double-dare *you!*

Andrew's stringy brown hair sticks out in weird clumps. Whenever Andrew thinks hard about something, he rubs his head. So his hair is always a mess, because he never stops thinking.

"Friends of yours?" Grandma murmurs. "I must meet them."

"Okay." You lean back out the window. "Yo! Guys!" you yell. You're about to tell them to come upstairs when Grandma grasps your arm.

"Not now!" she orders. "I need to freshen up after my travels. Unpack. Maybe take a nap."

You rub your arm where she grabbed you. She's one tough grandma!

Turn to PAGE 120.

"EMPLEH!" you tell Grandma excitedly. "It's HELP ME spelled backwards."

Grandma stares at you.

"Grandma!" You tug at her sleeve. "We have to go back! Someone on the train needs our help!"

"Oh, Cookie." She sighs. "I didn't want to have to do this so soon. But you give me no choice. I can't allow you to interfere with my mission."

Grandma pulls a small laser device from her pocket. She points it at you.

ZAP!

"Take me to your mother's rose garden," she orders.

You can't resist. You lurch forward and climb into a cab like a zombie. As soon as you arrive at your house, Grandma races to the rose garden.

"My eggs!" she cries. "My babies are ready to hatch!"

You stand by watching helplessly as Grandma digs up hundreds of alien eggs.

Turn to PAGE 45.

Before you can shoot, the spidery creature speaks. In perfect English!

"Thank you for rescuing us," it chirps.

"You're — you're . . . welcome!" you stammer.

"Your 'grandma' is an evil alien who kept us captive," the creature explains. "You have released us from our prison shells. We owe you our lives. We will never leave you!"

Say what?

Special Agent Bendrey rushes out of your house.

"While you were keeping an eye on the eggs, we snuck in and captured Grandma," he tells you. "She's in custody now. Thanks for your help." He dashes off.

"Wait!" you call after him.

Too late. He's gone. You never got to ask him one very important question.

How are you going to explain the dozens of alien houseguests to your parents?

Well, your mom is always telling you to make more friends. . . .

THE END

You can't go home without your grandma. Even if you feel as if you're in the middle of an earthquake.

You clutch the information counter to keep from falling over. You smile at the clerk, hoping to mask your fear.

"Train coming!" the clerk informs you, shouting over the noise. "Every time one comes in, this old station rattles like a baby's toy."

"I knew that," you fib. You hope the clerk doesn't notice how white your knuckles are.

The rattling stops with a loud screech of brakes. You make your way out onto the platform just as the doors to the train open. Mobs of people push their way out the doors.

You scan the crowd, searching for an old lady in yellow pants and a purple shirt. No luck.

"Hey, what are you doing here?" a voice calls.

Turn to PAGE 4.

Become an official investigator of aliens?

"You bet!" you exclaim. Ginny and Chuck nod enthusiastically.

"Great!" Grandma beams at you. "I'm going to go after Mithra-Dithra. But I need you to stay on this train."

You try to hide your disappointment. "Can't we go with you to defeat the evil alien?" you ask.

Grandma shakes her head. "I need you to track another set of aliens. You see, I discovered why there are so many aliens on this train. They're all heading for a big meeting a few miles up."

Chuck lets out a low whistle. "Like some kind of alien convention?" he asks.

"In a way." Grandma smiles. "They meet every few years on a centrally located planet. This year, they're coming to Earth."

Ginny shudders. "To do what?"

Grandma leans forward. "That's what I need you three to find out!"

Arrive at the alien meeting on PAGE 38.

"Ginny!" you shout. "Look out!"

Ginny scrambles over a pile of smashed suit-cases. She trips on a broken crate and sprawls on the floor. "Help me!" she shrieks.

The yellow-eyed thugs stalk closer.

Chuck crawls along the luggage rack, hurling down the few remaining boxes. The creatures are inches from Ginny.

You have to help her! You swing your legs over the side of the rack and drop to the floor. "Leave her alone!" you scream.

The door behind you flies open. The conductor bursts in.

Great! You might have a chance now.

"Help us!" you beg the startled conductor. "You've got to help us, please!"

Your heart stops as his head explodes! Right in front of you!

Scream in terror all the way to PAGE 40.

You, Sophie, and Andrew run out of the garage.

"We did it!" Sophie cries. "We actually captured an alien!"

"We'll be heroes!" Andrew crows.

But you can't join in the celebration. You've just thought of something. Something terrifying.

Sophie and Andrew dance around on the lawn. Then they notice your face.

"What's wrong with you?" Andrew demands. "We had a great plan and it worked perfectly. We got the alien!"

"Yes, we did," you say slowly. "But there are still all of those." You point to the rose garden.

The rose garden filled with purple pulsing eggs.

"Grandma called the roses her babies!" you explain. "Those must be her alien children. And I think they're about to hatch!"

Sophie gasps. "If they hatch, we'll be totally outnumbered."

"Should we call the authorities right now?" you ask them. "Or do we figure out something to do with the eggs?"

Andrew and Sophie don't say a word. They just stare at you.

So it's up to you.

Call the authorities on PAGE 49.
Deal with the eggs on PAGE 115.

You can't believe what this creature is saying. Your grandmother — an alien? No way!

The creature that used to be the conductor squeezes you tighter in its tentacles. Pieces of its human disguise drip down its uniform. "Now that we have the child, perhaps Mithra-Dithra will be more cooperative," it says.

"Who's Mithra-Dithra?" you ask.

One of the thugs makes a sound you assume is an alien laugh. "Your grandmother has taught you well."

"Yes," the other thug agrees. "But we won't be fooled. And your grandmother, Mithra-Dithra, will not succeed in her evil plan to rule this solar system."

"I don't know what you're talking about!" you yell. "My grandmother's first name is Susan, not Mithra-Dithra."

"You've made a mistake!" Ginny protests. "Just because the old lady dresses funny, it doesn't mean she's an alien!"

The three creatures fix their yellow eyes on you. They make that weird laughing noise again.

"You will answer our questions soon enough. Now we must prepare."

Prepare for what?

Find out what they plan to do with you on PAGE 83.

You, Ginny, and Chuck arrive at the alien meeting. Grandma has given each of you a disguise. You think your two blue heads look really cool!

But, unfortunately, this assignment turns out to be totally boring.

It really *is* a convention. These aliens get together to vote on galaxy parking rules, real estate taxes, and planetary trade pacts.

It's so dull, both of your blue heads fall asleep. The five-armed orange security guard has to throw you out. Your snoring is disturbing the guest speaker.

Oh, well. Sometimes even aliens turn out to be dull in

THE END.

"Let's get on board," you say. "We'll track down a conductor."

You, Sophie, and Andrew board the train. You slide open the door and enter the first car.

And stop.

A chill of horror runs along your spine. Your fingers tremble with fear.

"They're — they're —" Andrew stammers.

"Ghosts!" you whisper.

The train car is filled with shimmering figures, each more horrifying than the last. Heads float by without bodies. Bodies float by without heads. Skeletons move up and down the aisle. Wispy, cloudy girls and boys hover a few inches off the ground.

You reach for the door handle. It won't budge! And the train begins to move!

"We're trapped!" you shriek.

If only you had stayed home and listened to Special Agent Bendrey. Because compared to these ghouls, an alien is nothing!

And now you're stuck on this train going nowhere.

That is, nowhere *you* want to go!

Let's put it this way: Now that you're on the ghost train, this adventure has definitely come to

THE END.

"Aaahhhhhhh!" you shriek in horror.

Chuck falls to the ground, shaking with fear. Ginny sinks into the pile of bags.

You can't tear your eyes away from the terrifying sight. Flesh-colored globs splat onto the floor. Pieces of the conductor's face dangle around his neck.

But even more revolting is the disgusting new head that rises from his conductor's collar. A hairless, misshapen skull with lidless eyes. Yellow eyes. The size of ping-pong balls.

Tentacles shoot out from his sleeves. One wraps around your arm. The other grabs Ginny. A third bursts from the center of his chest. Right through the conductor's uniform. It yanks Chuck to his feet.

The tentacle is working its way up your arm toward your face. You've got to do something! But what?

If you haul off and punch the creature with your free hand, turn to PAGE 67.

If you bite the tentacles as hard as you can, turn to PAGE 47.

"It's more than Grandma's weird behavior," you explain. "It's a feeling I have."

Andrew and Sophie laugh. "Oh, excuse me," Sophie teases. "I didn't realize you had a *feeling!*"

"We all know how reliable those *feelings* are!" Andrew adds.

"Guys!" You run your hands through your hair. "I'm serious."

"Don't freak," Sophie consoles you with a laugh. "We think you're nuts, but we'll still help you."

"Yeah!" Andrew nods. "Spying will be fun! What's the plan?"

Plan? You haven't thought of one yet. You gaze out the kitchen window at Grandma in the garden.

"Maybe we should watch Grandma and try to figure out what she's doing in the rose garden," you suggest.

"Okay." Andrew and Sophie head for the door.

Then you have another idea. "Or maybe we should search her room."

Andrew and Sophie gaze at you. "She's *your* grandmother," Andrew says. "Make up your mind."

You heard Andrew. Choose!
Spy on Grandma in the garden on PAGE 79.
Search her room on PAGE 53.

You glance at Bendrey.

Your mouth drops open in horror.

By the bright light of the meteor rays you can clearly see Special Agent Bendrey. He's transforming in front of you!

Stalks shoot out from his face. Clusters of eyeballs dangle from the stalks! His head becomes a massive skull, as his human skin slithers off and drips to the ground.

"Nooooo!" Sophie shrieks.

You're too terrified to make a sound.

Or to run.

Three creatures exactly like Bendrey burst through the train car door. They quickly drag you and your friends inside.

"Sorry," Bendrey apologizes to the other creatures. "I tried to get back before the meteors hit, but these kids delayed me."

"No problem," one of the gross creatures responds. "We know just how to handle them." It grins.

When Special Agent Bendrey told you he was an alien investigator, he didn't mean he investigated aliens. He meant he was an *alien* who *investigated.*

Too bad you didn't investigate his story. Because now you're about to come to a gruesome

END!

The ground shakes so violently that you, Sophie, and Andrew are thrown down. You stay low, too terrified to move.

Dozens of miniature versions of the gross Grandma burst from the eggs. The purple flesh doesn't look any better baby-sized. If anything, you think, the young ones are *more* disgusting!

Grandma still hasn't seen you. All the newly hatched creatures line up in front of her.

"My children," she addresses them. "We have traveled to this galaxy to take over this world. You know what you must do. First, feed and grow. Next, fit yourselves out with human body parts." She holds up one of the rubber masks that you saw in her room earlier. "And then," she finishes with a hideous cackle, "go forth and carry out the Master Plan!"

You, Sophie, and Andrew all wear the same look of horror on your faces.

"We've got to stop them! Do you think we can fight them right here?" Sophie whispers.

"No way. Let's go tell my parents," Andrew urges. "We need help!"

To fight the aliens, turn to PAGE 88.
Tell Andrew's parents on PAGE 94.

"Let me help you with those." You reach for one of Grandma's two large suitcases.

Grandma shakes her head. "No, no. I'm perfectly balanced. If you take one I'll probably topple over." She giggles. "Now that would be a sight!"

You lead her out of the railroad station and to a taxi. Grandma shoves her suitcases into the trunk and then climbs into the cab beside you.

"Give the driver your address," she instructs, "and then tell me all about yourself."

You do as she says. But as you launch into a long story about your brilliant performance at school yesterday, she interrupts you.

"Tell me about the rose garden!" Grandma demands.

Try not to be annoyed and turn to PAGE 18.

Alien babies burst from the purple shells. They crawl everywhere, oozing yellow slime. Grandma dances around crazily.

"My plans to take over the universe will now come true!" Grandma cries. "My babies will be my army! No one will be able to stop us."

One little alien baby slithers over to you. It slides across your foot. It glances up and all five of its eyes gaze at you. It squeaks.

Hey!

It's kind of cute.

You pick it up. It makes a sound like a cat purring.

Oh, well. If aliens are going to rule Earth, it would probably be a good idea to have at least one alien on your side. Maybe then you won't come to such a terrifying

END.

Are you kidding?

You're turning down the chance to have a close encounter of the alien kind? You'd rather go home than spy on creatures from outer space?

Boy.

You sure aren't the kind of kid who usually reads GIVE YOURSELF GOOSEBUMPS.

Maybe you should go get your baby brother's nursery rhymes. Pick this book up again when you stop being such a wimp!

THE END

It would be useless to hit the powerful creature. Your fist is too small. It would feel like a gnat slugging an elephant.

But can you do it? Can you actually sink your teeth into that slimy tentacle?

You have no choice. It's wrapping around your throat.

You shut your eyes and chomp down on the squirming flesh.

Hmmm. Not bad. Kind of tastes like chicken.

You dig your teeth in deeper. The creature howls and drops Ginny and Chuck. You hang on with your teeth. Flailing tentacles smash into the walls and the ceiling. The two other creatures duck out of the way as the tentacles flip around.

CRASH! A strange-looking piece of equipment falls to the floor. The orange light instantly shuts off.

The ex-conductor's tentacles must have smashed the light that makes the force field, you realize. You glance at Grandma.

She blinks three times. She looks dazed.

The tentacled conductor-creature shrieks and writhes. But the two other creatures leap toward your grandma.

You release your teeth from the tentacle. "No!" you holler.

Turn to PAGE 95.

"My grandma is a special agent too?" You're so shocked, your voice squeaks.

"Exactly," Bendrey tells you. "We've been tracking an alien who we believe has assumed your grandmother's identity."

"Why would anyone impersonate my grandma?" Your head is spinning.

Bendrey shrugs. "To find out how much we know? To feed us false information? It could be anything."

"Why is the alien here?" Andrew asks.

"We're not sure," Bendrey replies. "The alien planted eggs in the rose garden here. We suspect they're about to hatch."

You shudder. Sophie's face has grown pale. Andrew looks like he's ready to throw up.

"I need your help," Bendrey continues. "We know where they've taken your grandma. The trouble is, the aliens who captured her know me. But *you* may be able to sneak into their headquarters."

Your mouth suddenly goes dry. "Me?" you choke out.

"Or," Bendrey goes on, "you can keep an eye on the eggs."

Both choices sound terrifying. But you have to pick one!

Help find Grandma on PAGE 20.
Spy on the alien eggs on PAGE 17.

"The eggs can wait," you decide. "We don't know how long that badminton net will hold Grandma. We should turn her over to the authorities before we do anything else."

You, Sophie, and Andrew head back into the house. You grab the phone in the kitchen. You pause, uncertain. "Who do I call?" you ask.

"No alien hotline in the phone book, huh?" Sophie jokes.

"My mom says to call 911 if there's an emergency," Andrew suggests.

"An alien in the garage qualifies as an emergency," you declare. You punch in the numbers.

Unfortunately, the emergency operator doesn't believe you. When she stops laughing, she scolds you for tying up the line. "Someone could be trying to phone in a *real* emergency!" she reprimands you.

"This *is* a real emergency!" you insist. But it's too late. She's already hung up.

You slam down the phone. "Now what?" you mutter.

Turn to PAGE 22.

You've entered the baggage compartment. But luggage isn't what has the three of you frozen in place, eyes wide.

Your grandmother sits on a chair surrounded by suitcases. She gazes straight ahead, unblinking. A strange orange light beams down onto her. She doesn't move. And although her eyes are open, she doesn't seem to see you.

"Is she ... is she ... you know ... ?" Ginny stammers.

"I can't tell," you reply. "I *think* she's alive, but ... "

"I know a way to find out!" Chuck says. He jumps up and down, puts his fingers up his nose, and howls in Grandma's ear.

No reaction from Grandma. You swallow hard.

"Wait. She *is* alive!" Ginny murmurs, creeping closer. "I can see her breathing."

"Then why doesn't she say something?" you worry aloud.

"Maybe she's under some kind of spell," Ginny whispers.

"Maybe it's this weird light," Chuck suggests. He waves a hand into the orange beam.

POW! Chuck's body flies across the railroad car. He lands in a crumpled heap on top of a suitcase.

Find out if Chuck is okay on PAGE 77.

"The alien is an impostor!" you exclaim. "She's done something with my real grandma. We have to save her!"

You explain to Sophie and Andrew about seeing the other woman on the train.

"We have to go back to the train station." You start climbing out of the tree house.

"Do you really think she'll still be there?" Sophie asks.

The question stops you. You cling to the tree trunk.

Maybe going to the train station *is* a dumb idea. But it's the only idea you have. "What else can we do?" you demand. "At least it's a place to start."

You scurry the rest of the way down and land with a soft thud on the grass. Sophie and Andrew drop down beside you. The three of you sneak around the side of the house. No sign of Grandma!

You dash across your front lawn.

CRRRRCKKK!

You glance up. Something moved in that tree!

Who — or what! — made that sound? Find out on PAGE 6.

You rush to Grandma #1 and assume a martial-arts position just like hers.

"How could you, Cookie?" Grandma #2 wails. "Why would you choose that fiend over me, your sweet ol' grandma?"

"My parents told me my grandma was unusual," you explain. "And full of surprises."

"That certainly describes me!" Grandma #1 boasts.

"And I don't think my real grandma would call me that terrible nickname. Especially since I'm not a little kid anymore!" you finish.

Ginny and Chuck slap high fives. "Way to go!" Chuck cheers.

"Sorry," Grandma #1 tells the other Grandma. "But don't feel too bad about not being believed. The original is always better than the copy."

Huh? What's she talking about?

Before you can ask, three more women charge through the door.

More Grandmas!

Turn to PAGE 8.

"This would be a good chance to find out more about Grandma," you tell Sophie and Andrew. "Let's search her room."

"Right, chief." Sophie salutes you.

You all trudge up to Grandma's room. The door is shut.

Glancing around, you quickly turn the doorknob. Then the three of you slip inside.

You gaze around the room. It just looks like an ordinary bedroom.

Andrew fidgets beside you. "We should hurry," he urges. "I don't want to get caught in here."

He's right.

But where do you begin?

To search the closets, turn to PAGE 62.
To look under the bed, turn to PAGE 76.

"Is something wrong?" a voice asks behind you.

You turn and face your grandmother standing on the platform. She and the woman on the train could be twins! What's going on?

Is this woman really your grandmother? Or is your *real* grandmother in terrible trouble on the train?

"Shouldn't we be getting a taxi, Cookie?"

You stare at her. Could you have made a mistake?

"All aboard," the conductor shouts. The train lets out an exhausted wheeze, then slowly pulls forward.

You could jump on the train now and find out if the woman in danger is your real grandma. Or you could assume the woman standing in front of you is the right woman. After all, she recognized you — and you didn't get a good look at the woman on the train.

It's now or never. What are you going to do?

If you leap aboard before the train pulls out, turn to PAGE 110.

If you believe you found the right Grandma, go to PAGE 26.

"Stay away from her!" the new Grandma warns. "She's evil!"

"Don't listen to her," the other Grandma yells. "She's an impostor!"

Your head spins. Ginny's gaze shoots back and forth between the identical Grandmas. Chuck stares with his mouth open so wide you can see the rubber bands on the inside of his braces.

Grandma #1 — the one who fought the three creatures — leaps into her martial-arts stance again. "Don't mess with me," she snarls.

The new Grandma — Grandma #2 — cowers by the door to the baggage compartment. "Oh, no!" she whimpers. "She's going to get me. She'll get all of us!"

"Shut up, you fake!" Grandma #1 snaps. "These kids are too smart to fall for your act. Right?"

She gazes straight at you.

Which Grandma is your grandma?

If you think Grandma #2 is your real grandma, turn to PAGE 23.

If you choose Grandma #1, turn to PAGE 52.

"Refrigeration is the way to go," you decide.

You, Sophie, and Andrew gather up the eggs. It takes you each three trips to get them all into the house.

By eating the leftover plate of chicken, throwing out the brussels sprouts, and rearranging the milk and juice, you manage to fit all the eggs into the refrigerator. By the time you're done, it's dark outside.

"Uh, guys," you say to Sophie and Andrew. "Not that I'm scared or anything, but would you mind sleeping over?"

They must understand how you're feeling. They don't even tease you. They just exchange a nervous look and say yes.

The next morning the sun streams through your bedroom window. You stretch, wiggling your toes and fingers.

Then you freeze. Your heart pounds hard in your chest.

Noises. Noises downstairs.

Turn to PAGE 60.

"I've got an idea," you whisper.

You outline your plan to Chuck and Ginny. "Wait for my signal," you say. They nod.

You grab a small box lying beside you and toss it to the other side of the compartment. The creatures' heads whip around. Their bodies tense and they move toward the noise.

"Now!" you shout. You and Chuck jump up and grab the rungs of the overhead luggage rack. With a grunt, you swing up onto the rack. Bags and boxes tip over, landing on top of the thugs.

Chuck clambers up beside you. Together you bury the creeps with luggage. Ginny pelts them with parcels and bags.

"We're winning!" you cry. "Keep throwing!"

Suitcases burst open as they hit the ground. Clothes fly everywhere. Bottles shatter and tubes ooze, spilling their contents all over the floor. But even in the chaos, your grandma sits staring straight ahead, imprisoned by the orange light.

"Rrrraaagghhhhhhh!" With a deafening roar the creatures explode out of the pile of luggage. They head straight for Ginny.

"Oh, no!" you shriek. Your eyes dart along the empty luggage racks. "We've run out of ammunition!"

Hurry to PAGE 35.

"Look at this!" you whisper.

Sophie and Andrew pop their heads up over the side of the tree house.

Grandma holds up another throbbing purple egg. She puts her free hand in her mouth. When she pulls it back out her index finger has turned lime green! A metal tip as sharp as a pin extends where her nail should be.

That's not a human finger, you realize.

Grandma sticks the metal tip into the pulsing egg. It throbs faster. Then it glows, as if it were lit up from inside.

Satisfied, Grandma lays the egg back down on the ground. Then she moves onto the next rose bush. Soon she makes her way through the entire garden and heads back to the house.

Andrew and Sophie stare at you.

"I hate to have to say this . . . ," Andrew begins.

"Your grandma is — she's, I mean, I think —" Sophie tries.

You nod miserably. "I know," you say. "My grandma is an alien!"

Turn to PAGE 69.

"No way are we going to miss out on an adventure like this!" Ginny finishes for Chuck.

"Great!" you cry. You quickly explain that you were about to check out the train cars in the direction the thugs dragged your grandma. Or the Grandma-impostor. Whoever.

"What are we waiting for!" Chuck urges. "Let's go!"

The three of you hurry into the next car. And then the car after that. And then the car after that.

"Are you sure of what you saw?" Ginny asks. "I mean, why would two tough guys go after somebody's grandmother?"

"Maybe it was just a coincidence that the two ladies were wearing the same clothes," Chuck adds.

"No! I know what I saw!" you insist. But inside, you wonder the same thing.

You arrive at the last car. On the door is a yellow sign with large black letters: NO ENTRY.

You notice Ginny and Chuck exchange a worried look. Before they can change their minds about helping you, you yank open the door. The three of you pile into the car.

You gasp, stunned by the shocking sight in front of you.

What's going on? Find out on PAGE 50.

60

You leap out of bed, trying to avoid stepping on Sophie and Andrew in their sleeping bags. "Wake up!" you whisper. "There's something moving around downstairs."

Sophie's eyes widen. "Grandma!"

"The eggs!" Andrew gulps.

You, Sophie, and Andrew sneak downstairs. You huddle outside the kitchen door. "On three," you instruct them. "One. Two." Your voice shakes with fear."

You gulp. "Three!"

With a shout, the three of you charge into the kitchen.

Who's there? Turn to PAGE 90.

Wham! Your landing knocks the wind out of you. You roll several yards. You can feel every rock through your clothes.

As you struggle to get up, you notice Grandma is already on her feet. She's speaking into her watch! You dash over. She smiles.

"We'll be out of here in no time!" she tells you.

Within minutes a helicopter is hovering over you. Your hair whips in the wind created by the rotating blades.

A rope ladder is tossed down. Grandma grabs a rung and scrambles up. You follow a few feet behind her.

As Grandma nears the helicopter door, she stops.

"Uh-oh," she mutters.

You don't like the sound of that.

Turn to PAGE 121.

You stride to one of the closets. "This seems like a good place to start," you announce. You fling open the door.

And gasp!

"What is it?" Sophie asks, her voice trembling.

You turn to her, a terrified look on your face. "Grandma's other clothes are even uglier than her purple-and-yellow outfit!"

Sophie punches your arm. "That's not funny!"

Andrew laughs. "Yeah, it is!" He steps into the closet and pushes aside the row of clothes hanging from the rod.

And gasps.

You snort. "Andrew, we're not going to fall for that now!"

"It wasn't funny the first time!" Sophie adds.

"I'm not being funny," Andrew tells you. He points to the back of the closet.

You peer beyond him. There, sitting on the shelves, is a shoebox overflowing with . . . hands.

Human hands!

Turn to PAGE 118.

"She's seen us!" you yell. "We've got to get out of here!" You grab Andrew's hands and help him out of the snarl of roses. Sophie crawls out from under a bush.

"Everybody okay?" you ask.

"No permanent damage," Sophie replies. Andrew nods.

"Then let's move it!"

You turn to run. And trip over a tangle of roots. The bushes are so thick that you can't see Grandma. But you can hear her. She's come out of the house. She's just outside the garden.

You scramble to your feet. You push aside a clump of roses.

And come face to face with a pair of eyes.

Eyes in the middle of a big fat rose!

Yikes! Hurry to PAGE 103.

You land on the small platform between train compartments. You flail your arms as you struggle to regain your balance. Once you feel steady on your feet, you fling the door open.

Everyone stares at you as you enter the car. You nervously run a hand through your hair. You try to act as if jumping between the cars of a moving train is the most natural thing in the world.

You have a feeling you're not very convincing.

You hurry into the next car.

The struggling woman was several cars ahead. You head through the swaying train, planning to pick up the woman's trail from where you'd last seen her.

But maybe you're in over your head. Those thugs in dark glasses looked dangerous. Maybe you need help.

If you think you should tell someone what you saw, turn to PAGE 70.

If you want to follow the woman's trail yourself, turn to PAGE 80.

Grandma said she planted the roses during a meteor shower. But she never mentioned that a meteor landed in the garden!

Didn't she notice?

"Let's look for pieces of the meteor," Sophie suggests.

"I don't think we'll be able to recognize meteor fragments," you caution her. "They'll just look like regular rocks."

"We should search anyway," Sophie insists.

You know better than to argue with Sophie.

You, Andrew, and Sophie head out the back door.

You're surprised to see Grandma kneeling in the rose garden. She's changed out of her purple-and-yellow outfit into an even stranger one — a shiny silver jumpsuit.

"I thought she was taking a nap," you murmur.

"Is that your grandmother?" Andrew asks.

"I think so. . . ," you answer uncertainly.

Sophie laughs. "What do you mean? Don't you know your own grandmother?"

Right now, you're not so sure. . . .

Turn to PAGE 75.

There's barely room under the bed for all of Grandma's things *and* the three of you. But somehow you fit.

"You're squashing me!" Sophie complains.

"Shh!" you hiss.

From under the bed, you can see Grandma's shoes enter the room. She kicks them off. Then she moves to a corner of the room you can't see. But you can hear her humming to herself.

A moment later you see a bizarre sight!

You still hear Grandma. But what you *see* is a long, purple, scaly tail!

You're so startled, you gasp.

Sophie and Andrew immediately clap their hands over your mouth.

Did Grandma hear you? Turn to PAGE 11.

No way! You're not putting that slimy tentacle in your mouth. Instead, you punch the creature's face with all your strength.

"Yeeoowwwwww!" you yelp. That hurt!

The creature doesn't even blink. It wraps you, Ginny, and Chuck even tighter in its tentacles.

"Alien being," one of the other yellow-eyed creatures addresses you. "We have come to destroy your evil grandmother's eggs. We have tracked her through the galaxy for thirty years, hoping she would lead us to her nest."

Ginny gasps. "'Through the galaxy'?" she echoes. "They—they're saying that they're aliens!"

Your head spins. That's not all. They're saying something even more unbelievable!

"Wh-what?" you sputter. "Are you saying *my grandmother* is an alien?"

Turn to PAGE 37.

You wait.

Nothing happens.

Phew! You let out your breath. The creatures must have left. You're safe.

"Are you okay?" Chuck asks, rushing over. You sit up and untangle the packing twine that wraps around your ankle.

"We better move fast," Ginny warns. "That crash was really loud. Someone might come to see what it was."

"Yeah," Chuck agrees. He helps you lift the mirror back upright. Luckily, it didn't break. "So how are we going to break through the orange force field and grab your grandma?"

You scratch your head. "Hmmmmm," you murmur. Then the mirror gives you an idea.

How will a mirror help you? Find out on PAGE 71.

You sit in silence, too stunned to think.

"Shouldn't we do something?" Sophie asks finally.

"Yes!" Andrew chimes in. "Let's call the police!"

"And tell them what?" you demand. "There's an alien in my yard digging up purple eggs and poking them with a green fingernail?" You snort. "Would *you* believe that story?"

"I guess not," Andrew admits.

"I know what we have to do!" Sophie says. "We have to capture your grandma. Then we'll torture her until she spills her guts!"

Whoa! Is Sophie serious? Turn to PAGE 114.

Those thugs looked dangerous, you decide. You need help.

You glance around the train car. Three kids reading comic books. A fat man sleeping. A teenage girl doing homework. Not much to choose from.

You approach the teenage girl. "Excuse me," you whisper. "I need your help."

The girl doesn't look up. "I'm busy!" she snaps.

You try again. "I saw a fight. And I —"

"Look!" She sighs. "I have an A average. I'm not going to blow it by messing up on this exam. Go away!"

Well, that was useless.

"Did you say you saw a fight?"

You turn at the sound of the deep voice. Looming over you is a man in an overcoat and sunglasses.

"Fight? Fight?" you babble. "Oh, uh, yeah. Last night. A boxing match on TV!"

You can't see the man's eyes behind his sunglasses. You're not sure if he believes you. But he nods and walks away.

You head toward the end of the car, searching for someone to help you. As you pass the bathroom, the door pops open. An arm reaches out and yanks you inside.

Turn to PAGE 72.

"Help me with this thing," you instruct Chuck and Ginny. Together, the three of you unwrap the large mirror. Then you carry it over to your frozen grandma.

"If we find the right angle," you explain, "we should be able to deflect the beams of the force field."

"What are you doing in here?" a voice demands behind you.

Your head whips around.

They're back! The two thugs in overcoats and sunglasses!

Think fast! Turn to PAGE 128.

You're shocked when you discover who dragged you into the tiny bathroom.

"Grandma!" you exclaim.

She claps her hand over your mouth. "Shhhh!" she hisses.

You struggle to breathe. She's incredibly strong.

"I'm going to take my hand away," she tells you. "Do you promise to be quiet?"

Your lungs feel as if they're about to explode. You nod.

"Good." Grandma releases you. "Sorry about that. But we can't risk being found."

"Who are those guys?" you demand. "Why are they after you?"

Grandma sighs. "I guess you need to know. You're in up to your neck, right along with me."

Yikes!

Listen to Grandma on PAGE 91.

"We better try to capture the alien," you decide. "It's the only way we'll be able to get someone to believe us."

"And help us," Andrew adds with a shudder. "But how?"

"There are three of us and only one alien," Sophie points out. "Maybe we can knock her out and lock her up."

It's the best idea anyone can come up with. "You two hide in the garage," you instruct your friends. "I'll find some way to lure Grandma there. Then you'll jump her. That way, we have surprise on our side."

"Sounds good," Andrew says. Sophie nods in agreement.

The three of you rush to the garage. You drum your fingers on the door, trying to think of a way to get Grandma to follow the plan.

What would attract Grandma's attention? you wonder. Then it hits you. The roses! Of course! She'll definitely come running if something threatens her precious roses.

You grab the garden hose and turn it on full blast. Then you drag the spurting hose out to the rose garden. You shove it into a large bush. Water sprays everywhere.

"Grandma!" you shout. "Come quick! The roses are drowning!"

Will Grandma fall for your plan? Find out on PAGE 16.

You poke your head up and peer over the trunks.

Two thugs in overcoats and sunglasses enter the baggage car. The same guys you saw fighting with your grandma!

Yikes! Did you say "guys"? When they remove their dark glasses you discover they aren't "guys" at all! Not *human* guys, anyway.

Their eyes! They're the size of ping-pong balls and glow a creepy yellow. Like lizards, they have no eyelids.

Chills of terror make your fingers and toes tingle.

You slink back down behind the trunks. "We're in terrible danger," you whisper to Ginny and Chuck.

Chuck gulps. "Let's wait until they leave, then grab your grandma and scram," he urges.

"How are we supposed to grab her through the force field?" Ginny demands. "It almost fried you."

"Then maybe we should overpower those creeps," Chuck suggests. "There are two of them and three of us."

Chuck and Ginny can't agree. They want you to decide.

If you attack the yellow-eyed creatures, turn to PAGE 57.

If you wait until they leave so you can free Grandma from the orange beam, turn to PAGE 87.

You stare at the woman in the rose garden. The woman who claims to be your grandmother. You think back to the train station. Your mother's strange phone call.

Could the Grandma in the garden be an impostor?

"She looks cool!" Sophie interrupts your thoughts. "Introduce us."

Maybe you should tell Sophie and Andrew your suspicions. They can help you keep an eye on her. Try to figure out if she's who she says she is.

Or maybe you're just being silly! After all, why would anyone impersonate your grandmother?

And she did say she wanted to meet your friends.

If you introduce Andrew and Sophie to Grandma, turn to PAGE 84.

If you spy on her first, turn to PAGE 78.

You kneel down to peer under the bed. "No wonder Grandma's suitcases were so heavy," you remark. "There's a lot of junk under here."

Sophie and Andrew help you drag stuff out from under the bed. But you can't figure out what any of it is! Strange boxes that don't seem to open. Bottles filled with strange liquids. You examine something that looks like a laptop computer. The keys have weird squiggles instead of letters.

The only things you recognize are the two empty suitcases.

"What *are* these things?" Sophie asks. You shake your head. You reach for the computer-like object.

And freeze!

Footsteps!

Hide under the bed on PAGE 66.

"Chuck!" you shriek. You race to his side. He's out cold.

Ginny kneels beside you. "What happened to him?" she cries.

"The orange light. It must be a force field of some kind," you answer. "That's why Grandma can't move."

Ginny's frightened eyes meet yours. "What are we going to do now?" she asks.

You wish you knew what to tell her.

"Whoa, what happened?" Chuck murmurs. His eyes blink open. "Who hit me?"

You and Ginny help him to his feet. "It wasn't a 'who,'" you explain. "It was a 'what.'" You point to the orange force field.

"I never knew light could feel so solid." Chuck rubs his face groggily.

"We better keep out of sight while we decide what to do," you suggest. "No telling who'll come in."

Chuck and Ginny nod their agreement. The three of you duck behind a set of large trunks.

Just in time.

You hear the door slide open.

Turn to PAGE 74.

Grandma makes you nervous. You want to find out more about her.

"I'll introduce you later," you tell Sophie and Andrew. "Right now, there's something you need to help me with."

You lead them back into the house. Sitting at the kitchen table, you quickly describe all the strange things you've noticed about Grandma since she's been here.

Sophie snorts. "So your grandmother is stronger than you. What's the big deal?"

"And my mom is always mixing up words," Andrew adds. "Half the time she calls me by my sister's name. So what if your grandma said *eggs* instead of *seeds*?

You sigh. They don't believe you.

Turn to PAGE 41.

"Let's find out what Grandma's doing in the garden," you say.

"Won't she notice us?" Andrew asks.

You gaze out the kitchen window. "The tree house!" you exclaim. "We can spy on her from there."

Sophie slaps you a high five. "Great plan!"

You, Sophie, and Andrew dart out the door. You scurry up the tree trunk. At the top you pull yourself onto the platform. Andrew and Sophie flop down beside you on the weathered planks.

You peer down at Grandma. She moves slowly through the rows of roses, stopping at each one.

Sophie fakes a yawn. "Wake me when something exciting happens."

Grandma kneels beside a rose bush and gently brushes soil away from the roots. Then, very carefully, she brings something up from under the ground.

A huge purple egg!

You gasp. Grandma *did* plant eggs in the rose garden!

The large purple egg in her hand pulses as if it were breathing. As if it were getting ready to burst from the shell!

Turn to PAGE 58.

You have a funny feeling no one would believe you if you said you have twin grandmas and one's in trouble on the train.

You're not even sure if *you* believe you!

You decide to investigate on your own.

You continue through the moving train. You arrive at the compartment with the message in the window. It's smeared, but traces of the red letters are still there.

You aren't crazy, after all.

You search the seat for clues. A lost wallet. Or luggage. Anything to prove the woman's identity.

But you find nothing.

You get to the door at the far end of the car and reach for the handle.

A heavy hand lands on your shoulder.

"Where do you think you're going?" a gruff voice demands.

Uh-oh. Who has you in such a strong grip? Quick! Flip to PAGE 89.

The alien bends over, opens its mouth, and vomits out a slimy, snarling, dog-like monster.

"Meet Fido," the yellow-eyed creature says with a laugh.

Fido snarls. It has three rows of razor-sharp teeth. Its fangs drip with slime.

"I can't tell you anything! I don't know what you're talking about!" you gasp.

"Perhaps your friends will be more cooperative." The two other aliens each vomit out a drooling dog.

Fido lunges at you. The other monster-dogs leap at Chuck and Ginny.

"It's hurting me!" Chuck screams. "Tell them!"

You desperately push the monster-dog away. You're almost too terrified to think. Should you just tell them your address? You know your grandmother isn't this evil Mithra-Dithra, so what difference would it make?

But once you give the creatures what they want, won't they go ahead and kill you? They won't need you anymore.

Decide quick! Fido's drool burns your skin like acid!

Tell the aliens where you live on *PAGE 99*.

Bluff and think of some way to stay alive on *PAGE 107*.

"In here!" you hiss. You, Andrew, and Sophie pile into the closet. You yank the door shut behind you just as the bedroom door bursts open.

You can hear Grandma bustling about in the room.

Please don't look in the closet, you think over and over. Please don't look in the closet!

Sophie has her hand over her mouth. Andrew's eyes are shut.

After a few tense moments, you hear the door open and close again. You glance at Sophie and Andrew. Sophie shrugs. Andrew opens his eyes and nods.

You take a deep breath and open the door.

Turn to PAGE 127.

The conductor-creature snaps open a wall panel, revealing dials, knobs, and switches. Your grandma is still frozen in the force field. The conductor turns a dial.

The train car suddenly hums with a pulsing electronic sound. With a rumbling *WHOOSH* the baggage car releases from the train. It shoots in the opposite direction down the track.

"What's going on?" Chuck yells over the noise.

Before you can answer, the car lurches. You're thrown to the floor. In an instant, the baggage car lifts off the ground and hurtles into the sky.

"We're in some kind of spaceship!" you cry.

"Now that you realize there is no escape," the ex-conductor suggests, "perhaps you will be more cooperative."

"Tell us." The smaller alien approaches you slowly. "Where do you live? Where did your grandmother bury the eggs?"

"I don't know what you're talking about!" you protest.

"You'll change your story," the other creature warns. "We'll get the answer we want."

Then it does something so disgusting, you nearly faint.

What's so disgusting? Turn to PAGE 81. If you can stand it!

Stop being ridiculous, you scold yourself. What's the big deal about a silver jumpsuit? Your own mother wears mismatched socks and goofy hats.

"Come on," you tell Andrew and Sophie. "I'll introduce you."

The three of you stroll across the backyard to the rose garden. The flowers are unusually large, and have a strong odor. Almost sickeningly sweet.

"I've never seen roses that color before," Andrew says.

Come to think of it, neither have you. Blue roses? Striped roses? This is one weird rose garden.

Grandma stands as she sees you approaching. "Oh, goody," she gushes. "I enjoy meeting new people."

"Cool flowers," Sophie compliments Grandma.

"Thank you, dear," Grandma says. "Why don't you take a closer look?"

You, Sophie, and Andrew wander into the thicket of rose bushes. Some of them are so large, they tower over you. You gaze at a bright green rose.

Whoa!

Is that a pair of eyes staring back at you?

Gasp and turn to PAGE 103.

You have to find out what makes the suitcases weigh so much.

Then you have to find out how Grandma carried them so easily!

"Okay," you whisper to the cab driver. "But hurry!"

You glance around. No Grandma. Great! You figure she's still checking out her precious rose bushes.

The cab driver fiddles with the lock on the luggage. "Hmm," he murmurs. "I've never seen a lock like this before."

You bend down beside him. You examine the small lock on the suitcase. It glows blue and feels warm in your hand. It's not a combination lock, and it doesn't seem to have a slot for a key. "It *is* weird," you agree.

"Now I really want to get these bags open!" The cab driver laughs. "I can't resist a challenge!"

You peer closely at the lock. You notice a small rose etched into the metal.

"I wonder if . . ."

You press hard on the rose.

The lock snaps open!

Find out what's inside the suitcase on PAGE 105.

"Cookie! Cookie, over here!"

You shudder at hearing your old nickname. You *hate* that name! Luckily, Ginny and Chuck aren't around to hear it!

"Cookie!"

You turn toward the voice. At the end of the station you see a woman with white hair. She's waving wildly. No way to mistake her for anyone else. Not in those clothes.

You wave back, approaching her cautiously. Anyone who would call you "Cookie" is likely to pinch your cheeks too.

As you stroll down the platform, something catches your eye. Bright red letters scrawled across one of the train windows.

A message!

If your mother hadn't made that strange phone call, you wouldn't have thought twice about it. But now you have an odd feeling. . . .

Maybe the message is meant for you.

Read the message on PAGE 100.

"Those guys aren't human," you tell Ginny and Chuck. You shudder. "I don't want to try taking them on."

You, Chuck, and Ginny scrunch down as low as you can behind the trunks. You try to not even breathe.

Then you hear the door slide open again.

Have they left? you wonder. Or did someone else come in?

Only one way to find out.

You crawl between packing crates and boxes, searching for signs of the creatures. As you slide along the floor, something hooks around your ankle.

CRASH! A large, rectangular mirror wrapped in plastic thuds to the floor right behind you.

Oh, no! Did those yellow-eyed creatures hear you? Are you about to be zapped?

Hold your breath until PAGE 68.

"We have to stop them *now*," you whisper. "By the time we go for help, they could be anywhere!"

"Doing anything!" Andrew adds with a shudder.

But how can you stop them? you wonder. You watch the horrifying creatures, trying to think of an idea.

"Feed well," Grandma orders. "And then we must begin."

The slimy aliens swarm over the roses, munching everything in their path. Grandma strolls through the wriggling masses. You remember how she told them to feed and grow. You don't have much time. Whatever you do, it has to be fast and effective.

"Let's squash them!" you decide. "While they're all in the garden."

"Brilliant," Sophie replies. "How?"

Figure out an answer on PAGE 13.

You wriggle out of the hand's grasp and spin around.

The train conductor glares down at you.

Strange, you think. He's wearing dark glasses.

But what he says isn't strange at all.

"Ticket, please."

Oops. You forgot about needing a ticket.

Now what?

If you stall while you try to figure a way out of the situation, turn to PAGE 21.

If you explain to the conductor the real reason you're on the train, turn to PAGE 92.

You tear across the linoleum . . .

And smash right into your mom!

She shrieks and drops a plate of scrambled eggs. Your dad jumps up from the table, scattering his newspaper.

"Mom! Dad! What are you doing here?" you demand.

"I got an emergency call from work," Mom explains, cleaning up the mess. "That's what I told you on the phone at the train station, remember? So we cut our trip short. We just got in half an hour ago. We didn't want to wake you. Where's Grandma?"

You sneak a peek at Sophie and Andrew. "Uh— I guess she's still sleeping," you mumble.

Well, it might be true. Even if she *is* sleeping in the garage.

"Sit down, kids," your mom commands. "I made a huge breakfast."

Excellent! You, Sophie, and Andrew wolf down three big plates of scrambled eggs. Even your dad, who usually only has coffee in the morning, manages to finish a second helping.

"Funny," he says. "I can't stop eating these eggs."

You suddenly have trouble swallowing.

Turn to PAGE 109.

Grandma gazes solemnly at you. "I'm a secret agent," she informs you.

Your mouth drops open. "Y-y-you . . . what?" you sputter.

"It's true. Those men who grabbed me think I'm smuggling a special computer disk."

"Are you?" you blurt.

She smiles. "It's better if you don't know for sure."

You have a zillion questions you want to ask her. But a sharp knock on the bathroom door startles you. Grandma pulls a small, high-tech device from her pocket.

"What do you think we should do?" she whispers. "Should we take our chances and open the door? Or should we sneak out through the window?"

It's up to you.

If you climb out the bathroom window, turn to PAGE 97.

If you yank open the door, turn to PAGE 29.

"I'm not really a passenger on the train," you tell the conductor.

"Could have fooled me," the conductor responds.

"I mean, that is, uh . . ." You're having trouble explaining.

"Yes? This I have to hear." The conductor crosses his arms and peers down at you.

"I saw this fight. A woman struggling with two guys in sunglasses. And I think the woman was my grandma."

"Your grandma? In a brawl?" The conductor snorts in disbelief.

"But it's true!" you cry.

It's no use. He grabs your sleeve and yanks you to the door.

"That's the worst excuse for not paying a fare that I ever heard!" he declares. He lifts you up under the armpits and lowers you to the platform.

Luckily, the train hasn't picked up much speed yet. You only stumble a few steps.

"Cookie!" Your furious grandmother marches toward you. "What's gotten into you? Jumping on and off moving trains! That's it. You're grounded!"

Some way to start a vacation. Grounded! You can't wait until your grandmother's visit comes to an

END.

Sophie, Andrew, Andrew's parents — they're all aliens. You're the only human in the room!

You're too horrified to think of running.

Andrew reaches into his pocket and pulls out a squirming baby alien. He places it on your shoulder. "Feed and grow," he tells it.

Uh-oh.

As the baby alien nibbles at your ear, you think: Mom wouldn't let me get my ear pierced, but I got my way in the — OWWWWWWWW!

(END!)

"I don't want to face those creatures alone!" you say. "Let's go get help!"

The three of you half-crawl, half-stumble out of the backyard. The moment you reach the street, you take off running. You cover the three blocks to Andrew's house in record time.

"Mom! Dad!" Andrew yells as you charge through the front door. "Come quick!"

Andrew's parents step into the hallway from the dining room. "What's all the shouting?" his dad asks.

"Aliens!" you blurt. "There are aliens in my backyard!"

Andrew's parents stare at you. Then they start to laugh.

Oh, no! They don't believe you!

Convince them on PAGE 102.

"Grandma! Look out!" You race toward her.

But Grandma doesn't need any help! She leaps to her feet and assumes a karate stance. With a swift kick, she knocks one creature to the ground. It's out cold.

The other creature jumps her from behind. Grandma bends sharply at the waist and flips the creature over her back. It falls in a crumpled heap.

With a howl, the conductor-creature reaches for Grandma. But she's ready for it. She ducks, then grabs one of its tentacles. She jerks the creature hard and it tumbles over. In a smooth move, she uses the tentacles to tie all three creatures together.

Your mouth drops open in awe.

"Whoa!" You let out a long, low whistle. "Some action!"

"That was awesome!" Ginny agrees.

"Totally!" adds Chuck.

Grandma beams at you. She rubs her hands together. "That was fun!" she exclaims.

You stare at her.

Is this amazing woman really your grandmother?

Turn to PAGE 119.

You glance around, hoping for an idea. Your eyes land on a ladder leading to the top of the train.

"Up there!" You grab a rung and climb. At the top, you reach down and help lug up Grandma. Your muscles strain with the effort. Chuck and Ginny shove her from below as you yank her limp arms. Finally, you're all gasping on top of the train.

"We don't know how long that force field will hold," you warn. "We better keep moving."

The three of you drag Grandma across the cartops. It's tough going. You're not sure if this was such a good idea.

"I'll see if anyone is looking for us." You scurry to the side of the train. "Grab my ankles."

Ginny and Chuck grasp your ankles and lower you down headfirst. You peer into the train car window.

And gasp!

The train car is filled with people in sunglasses.

One of them notices you. He points and moves closer to the window. He pulls off his glasses to take a better look.

Yellow ping-pong-ball eyes!

Panic all the way to PAGE 111.

"Out the window," you declare. "Or we'll be trapped in here."

"Good choice," Grandma says. She slips the device back into her pocket. You peer out the window. The countryside speeds by.

There's nowhere to go out that window, you realize. Nowhere but down.

The pounding on the door increases. It strains on its hinges. No more time to waste.

"Remember—duck and roll," Grandma instructs you. She gives you a boost up.

Then you fling yourself out the window.

Duck and roll to PAGE 61.

You gaze at the startling scene through the window. Inside the train compartment a woman struggles fiercely with two men. The men wear tan overcoats and large, dark sunglasses.

But it's the woman who holds your attention.

A white-haired woman wearing yellow stretch pants and a purple shirt.

She's a dead ringer for your grandma!

The two thug-like men yank her under each arm and lift her out of the seat. Her terrified eyes lock onto yours as she is dragged roughly into the aisle. The men pull her toward the door at the far end of the car.

Hurry to PAGE 54.

Ginny's and Chuck's screams rip through you worse than the monster-dog's acid drool.

"Okay! Okay!" you shriek. "Call off the dogs!"

You rattle off your address.

"Very good." The three alien creatures lean over and open their jaws wide. The monster-dogs jump back into their mouths. The creatures swallow.

Then all three belch and pat their tummies.

Man. Talk about disgusting.

"We are terribly sorry," the ex-conductor says. "But we really did need to know. And now we'll take you home."

With the twist of a few dials, the spaceship changes direction. In minutes you land behind your house.

You glance out the window and gasp.

What has you so upset?

Rush to PAGE 104.

100

You gaze at the train window. You read the red letters aloud.

"Empleh. Empleh," you mutter. What does it mean? It doesn't sound familiar. Maybe it's not an English word.

That terrible nickname interrupts your thoughts.

"Cookie! I'm waiting for a big hug and kiss!"

Exactly what you were afraid of.

"Hi, Grandma." You stop several inches away from her. Just beyond her reach.

Wrong! Grandma throws her arms around you, squeezing you hard. So hard, you can barely breathe. Finally she releases you.

"Cabs are at the other end of the station," you gasp, trying to catch your breath.

Grandma follows behind you, chattering all the way. She asks about your school, your parents, and your mother's rose bushes.

On the way out of the station, you pass the train window with the message again.

I've got it! you think. I know what it means!

Do you really?

If you know what it says, turn to PAGE 14.

If you need help to figure it out, turn to PAGE 129.

"What's the problem?" you ask the struggling cab driver. "Skipped breakfast this morning?"

The cab driver glares at you. Sweat trickles down his forehead. "*You* try to lift those bags," he grunts.

You reach in and grab the handle of the top suitcase.

Whoa! That bag is heavy! You grit your teeth and yank hard. Every muscle strains as you lift the bag out of the trunk.

"I don't get it," you murmur. "Grandma carried both of those bags without any trouble."

"Then Grandma must be a weight lifter," the cab driver snaps.

Together, you half-drag, half-carry the luggage to the front door. You drop yours with a loud thud. "That must weigh two hundred pounds," you gasp.

The cab driver glances around. "Let's open them," he whispers. "I want to know what Grandma has that weighs so much!"

Hmm. You know it would be snooping. But you're dying of curiosity.

What are you going to do?

Open the suitcases on PAGE 85.
Tell the cab driver "No way" on PAGE 7.

"Come see!" you shriek. "There are dozens of them in my backyard! Andrew, tell them!"

But he doesn't say a word!

You turn to Sophie. "Sophie! You saw them! Tell them I'm not crazy."

You don't like the way they're all smiling at you. As if they were all in on a big joke.

"There are aliens trying to take over the world!" you shout. "Why won't you believe me?"

"We *do* believe you," Andrew's mother says in a soothing tone.

Then she peels off her face!

So do Andrew, Sophie, and Andrew's dad.

They look exactly like Grandma!

This is bad. Turn to PAGE 93 to see if there's a way out.

The eyes on the rose blink at you!

"Sophie! Andrew!" you choke out. "Run!"

But your warning comes too late. Long green tendrils wrap themselves around you and your friends.

"Noooo!" Sophie shrieks.

"What's happening?" Andrew screams.

You strain against the tight grip of the plant. "Grandma! Help us!" you cry.

But Grandma ignores you. She skips through the rose bushes, chanting. You're about to holler again when the rose spits a glob of slimy orange goo right into your face. It fills your mouth and eyes.

You wipe your face on your sleeve, but the sticky substance won't come off. It's too thick. You can't see a thing.

But you can hear Sophie and Andrew screaming for help. And Grandma reciting something. It sounds like a nursery rhyme!

You struggle to move toward your friends, but your feet are stuck. Is the plant wrapped around them? you wonder.

Then you realize the horrible truth. You no longer have feet. You have roots.

You're turning into a plant!

Turn to PAGE 113.

"Oh, no!" you wail. "You landed on my mom's petunias. They're totally ruined. My mom's going to go ballistic!"

But it gets worse. As soon as the spaceship hatch pops open, the creatures go to work. They dig up her prize rose bushes.

You are going to be in *big* trouble when your mom comes home.

You don't believe what you see next. You are soon ankle-deep in hundreds of enormous, pulsing purple eggs.

Your grandma must be an alien after all!

When the creatures have filled their ship with the eggs, the ex-conductor approaches you. "Now you understand why we must keep your grandmother. But we apologize for the mess," it says. "Here are some seeds to replace the plants we destroyed."

"Uh, thanks." You take the packet from the wiggling tentacle.

With a wave, the creature enters the spaceship. You watch it leave the atmosphere.

Chuck and Ginny help you with the garden. Alien flowers grow differently from Earth plants, you realize. Within minutes the garden is overflowing with gigantic roses.

Your mom should be pleased. As long as she doesn't mind roses that smell like bananas and glow in the dark!

THE END

The moment the lock pops open, the suitcase begins to vibrate.

You stumble backward, banging into the startled cab driver. He trips and the two of you tumble off the front step. You land hard on the lawn.

The suitcase spins around and around. As it bounces wildly, the sides slowly open. Purple mist escapes from the bag with a hissing sound.

"Wh-wh-what's going on?" the cab driver stammers.

But you can't answer him. You are too stunned by what you are seeing. With a *WHOOSH!* a giant rose bush bursts from Grandma's suitcase!

You scramble to your feet. The terrified cab driver is still sprawled on the ground directly below the huge rose bush. Grandma races around the corner of the house.

"Oh!" she calls. "I see you've found my prize plant."

You stare up at the dozens of giant flowers towering over you. Each bud is twice the size of your head. "But what—? How—?"

Grandma smiles. A strange, evil smile.

"How did it get so big?" she finishes for you. "My rose has a very special diet. And I think it's time for lunch!"

Find out what's on the menu on PAGE 117.

106

"This way!" You dash to the window, Andrew and Sophie right behind you. You yank it open and stick your head out.

The ground suddenly seems very faraway.

However, Grandma's footsteps are definitely very close!

"Try to land in the rose garden," you instruct your friends. "The bushes should help cushion the fall."

You climb out onto the window ledge. You shut your eyes, and take a deep breath.

Then you jump.

You land on a tall rose bush. Thorns poke you all over. You feel shaken up, but you aren't hurt. Andrew and Sophie leap down beside you.

You pull yourself out of the scratchy branches and plop onto the soft ground. You gaze up at the window.

Grandma smiles down at you.

A chilling, evil smile.

Then she vanishes back inside.

Turn to PAGE 63.

These creeps think you're related to a powerful alien. Maybe if you act powerful too, they'll be afraid of you.

"Call off your dogs!" you command. You try to sound like alien royalty. "Or I'll unleash my own forces."

The creatures glance at each other. One of them makes a shrill beeping sound. The vomit-dogs freeze in mid-bite.

Hah! This might work.

"Now that you have seen through my human disguise," you continue, "there's no point in pretending. I am Smithra-Schmithra—heir to the Mithra-Dithra kingdom."

Ginny and Chuck stare at you. This is fun!

"So stay back!" you bellow. "Or you'll feel my wrath!" You point at the three creatures.

Sparks shoot out of your fingers!

Huh? How'd you do that?

Turn to PAGE 116.

108

A chill runs through you. What was your mother trying to say? Is your grandmother in trouble? Is there danger at the station?

As you hand the phone back to the information clerk, the whole train station begins to rumble.

Could this be what your mother was trying to warn you about?

Should you get out of there and go home?

Or are you supposed to find your grandmother?

If you get out of there right away, turn to PAGE 12.

If you stay to find Grandma, turn to PAGE 33.

"Mom?" you ask. "Where did you get the eggs?"

You aren't happy when you hear the answer.

"From the refrigerator, silly," she tells you. She scoops up another forkful. "Did you buy them? They weren't there when we left."

You gaze at Sophie, then at Andrew. Then you stare down at your plate of food.

"Were they, uh, kind of unusual-looking?" you ask your mom.

"Come to think of it, they were rather large." She thinks for a moment. "And a strange color."

Your stomach does a flip-flop.

You've been eating the alien eggs!

Have you ever heard the expression, "You are what you eat"?

You're about to find out how true it really is!

THE END

110

You have to find out if that woman in trouble is your grandmother. Besides, you're dying to find out why those men in dark glasses were fighting with a little old lady—and having such a hard time!

The train starts to pull out of the station. You race down the platform, searching for a good spot to jump aboard. Your legs and arms pump hard, your muscles straining, as you match the speed of the train.

"COOKIE! Come back here! What are you doing?" Grandma's voice floats after you.

If I'm wrong, you think, and the woman on the train *isn't* my real grandma, I'm going to be in big trouble.

But you're not going to back out now.

You take a deep breath and leap!

Will you make it?

Land on PAGE 64.

"Pull me up! Pull me up!" you shriek. Ginny and Chuck lift you back on top of the train.

"They saw me! They know we're up here!" you yell. "They'll be after us any second!"

Ginny and Chuck stare at each other. Their faces are white with fear. Yours is too.

"We're going to have a hard time escaping with your grandmother like that." Chuck points to Grandma. She looks like a limp rag doll.

"We can't waste any time," you urge. You peek over the side of the train again.

And stare into a pair of yellow eyes gazing up at you.

One of the creatures is leaning out the window.

Do something! Fast!

If you leap from the train before it's too late, turn to PAGE 10.

If you wake Grandma so you can try to crawl away, turn to PAGE 28.

Grandma yanks the tape player out of Sophie's hands. She throws it to the ground. Andrew runs and trips, smashing the CD player. You're so scared, you drop the radio.

Silence.

Aliens swarm around you. Their teeth dig into your ankles.

Think of something! Try anything!

Maybe it wasn't sound waves that killed the creatures, you realize. Maybe it was music!

You sing the first words that pop into your head. "Happy birthday to you," you warble.

"Nooo!" Grandma shrieks again.

The aliens gnawing on your ankles fall over. Andrew and Sophie figure out what you're doing. They begin singing too.

After five choruses of "Happy Birthday," the garden is filled with dead aliens. You defeated them all. Even Grandma.

You, Sophie, and Andrew collapse to the ground.

"We did it!" you exclaim. "We stopped the alien invasion!"

"Now what do we do?" Sophie asks. "Do we tell someone?"

A broad grin spreads across your face. "I think we should form a singing group."

"What?" Andrew stares at you. "A singing group?"

"You bet," you reply. "We'd knock 'em dead!"

THE END

Panic rises in your chest, making it difficult for you to breathe.

"Grandma! Help!" you pant.

But it's no use. She continues to chant.

Your face twists. Your skin flakes, forming petals. Your arms flatten against your sides. Your body gets longer and thinner.

The whole time, Grandma goes on chanting. A chill runs through your mutated body. You finally realize what she's reciting.

It's a nursery rhyme, all right. But with some major changes in the words:

"Roses are red
Violets are blue
What you didn't know was . . .
The rose would be YOU!"

THE END

"Sophie!" You stare at your friend.

She grins. "Just kidding. About the torture part. But I do think we should capture your grandma."

A horrible thought hits you. "Oh, no!" you gasp. "If the woman in the garden is an alien, then the woman I saw at the train station must be my real grandmother!"

What should you do? Your real grandma is in danger. But you and your friends are in danger too! Maybe the whole world is in danger from the alien. You don't know why she's here!

Try to capture the alien Grandma on PAGE 73.
Try to find and rescue your real grandmother on PAGE 51.

"We better do something about the eggs," you decide. "I think Grandma will stay put for a while."

You, Sophie, and Andrew approach the rose garden. Dozens of large purple eggs lie scattered on the ground. They're not pulsing or glowing anymore.

"What do you think they are?" Sophie whispers.

"I don't know," you admit. "They could be alien food. Or alien flower bulbs . . ."

"Or little alien monsters waiting to hatch," Andrew adds.

You glare at him. "Thanks for pointing that out." You gaze back at the rows of roses, wondering what to do.

And you can't help noticing that it's getting dark.

"What if we stick them in the fridge?" Andrew tugs at his messy hair. "It would be too cold for them to hatch, and we can have them analyzed at a lab tomorrow."

"Or maybe we should squash them." You know it sounds harsh, but it might be the safest thing to do.

Which is it going to be? Squash the eggs on PAGE 126.

Refrigerate them on PAGE 56.

116

The sparks from your fingers short-circuit the orange force field around your grandmother.

Grandma shakes her head a few times. Then she smiles at you.

"Cookie!" she exclaims. "Good. I see you have everything under control. I knew I could count on you."

You wave your hand at the cowering yellow-eyed creatures again. Sparks fly at them. "Wh-wh-what's going on?" you stammer.

Grandma beams. "Awww," she coos. "My little baby is growing up. You've reached the age when you can use your powers."

Powers? So it's true?

You are an alien after all!

Your grandma is Mithra-Dithra. Together you take over the world.

You put Ginny and Chuck in charge of their very own solar systems. And you make the yellow-eyed thugs your galactic chauffeurs.

THE END

"Yes," Grandma croons. "I think my baby is hungry."

You gaze up at the huge rose bush. Could it be? Is it . . . moving?

Your heart pounds triple time. One of the enormous roses bends down toward the cab driver. In a flash, it gobbles him up. You shut your eyes. But you can still hear the cab driver's muffled screams.

Then — silence.

Trembling, you open your eyes.

Oh, no! The gigantic flower is inches from your head!

"Good, baby," Grandma coos. "You ate every bite of dinner. So now you get to have a nice treat for dessert!"

Eek!

You have a terrible feeling you know what dessert is going to be!

Well, what did you expect with a nickname like *Cookie*?

THE END

118

You reach toward the box of hands. Your stomach lurches, but you have to find out if they're real.

Your fingers gently poke at the flesh.

Rubber!

You let out a huge sigh. "They're fake!" you exclaim.

"That doesn't explain why they're here," Sophie points out.

Andrew searches the closet over by the window. "There are feet in this closet," he tells you.

Before you can go over to look, you hear footsteps on the stairs.

Grandma!

"Quick! We have to get out of here!" you whisper hoarsely. The footsteps are coming closer.

"If we leave now," Sophie says, "she'll see us!"

Sophie is right.

Your eyes desperately scan the room for a place to hide. Or a way out. Your gaze lands on the window.

Do you dare?

Or should you pop into the closet?

To go out through the window, turn to PAGE 106.
To hide in the closet, turn to PAGE 82.

"What a mess!" Grandma glances around the wrecked baggage car. "Help me find my suitcases. Then we can get out of here."

You spot a suitcase with your grandmother's name on it. The top is popped open. Papers slide out of it onto the floor.

"Found one!" you call. As you place the papers back into the suitcase, several files catch your eye.

TOP SECRET! CONFIDENTIAL! SPECIAL GOVERN-MENT DOCUMENTS! are stamped all over the files.

Grandma darts over and snatches the files out of your hands.

"Thanks," she says. She shoves the papers into the suitcase and snaps the lid shut.

You stare at her. What is your grandmother doing with secret government files?

You're about to ask her when the door flies open again.

"Thank goodness I found you before it's too late!" a voice cries.

It's the other Grandma!

Face the twin Grandmas on PAGE 55.

"Run along now," Grandma tells you.

You bound out of her room, downstairs, and out the back door. You hate to admit it, but your own grandmother gives you the creeps. You can't shake the feeling that something is very wrong.

Sophie and Andrew are sprawled on your back porch.

"Hey, guys," you greet them. "What's up?"

"We're hungry!" Sophie announces. "We need brownies."

Andrew nods. "Or we'll collapse before the big event."

"What big event?" you ask, leading them into the kitchen. You set a plate of Mom's fresh brownies on the table.

Sophie and Andrew are too busy munching to answer. Finally, Sophie swallows. "Milk," she croaks. "Give me milk!"

You grab the milk carton. You hold it over Sophie's head. "Tell me what the big event is," you insist. "Or I'll give you a milk shampoo!"

Andrew snorts. "How about a *milky way* shampoo?" He holds up a newspaper. "Check this out."

You grab the newspaper and scan the article. "Meteor shower tonight," you read aloud. "Cool!"

You peer at the tiny map. Then your eyes widen. "Hey! That's my house!" you sputter. "Fifteen years ago, a meteor crashed here. Right in our rose garden!"

Turn to PAGE 65.

"Jump," Grandma whispers down to you. "These aren't the good guys."

The helicopter is already lifting away. You glance at the ground below you. Yikes!

"Grab the disk out of my sock," Grandma continues. "Don't let them see you do it. Take it straight to the address on the label. You'll be safe there."

She has the special disk on her after all! Cool!

You slip the disk out of her sock. Grandma climbs up as if nothing is wrong. You take a deep breath and let go of the ladder.

After jumping from a moving train, this doesn't seem so bad. You land and take off running.

All this fuss over some stupid computer floppy! You dart into some bushes and examine the disk. The address on the label isn't too far from your house. You head off in the right direction.

Turn to PAGE 123.

"Hold it!" the reporter yelps. "I've got to change tapes. No way am I going to miss the story of the century!"

"Shut up!" you shout. You notice Andrew and Sophie hanging back in the doorway. Their eyes are wide open, staring at you. "It's a lie!" you wail at them.

"Cookie! How can you say that? Of course it's true." Grandma holds out her seven arms to hug you.

"This is great stuff!" the reporter cheers. "Child discovers alien identity. Alien confesses all! I see a promotion for me!"

At least *somebody's* happy here, you think.

Cheer up! Seven arms could come in handy. And maybe, if Grandma's movie is a big hit, she'll let you be her manager.

THE END

You sneak back toward home. You try to stay out of sight.

By the time you pass your house, you're pretty sure you're safe. You check the address on the computer disk again. You wonder what's on the disk. What makes it so valuable?

You can't resist. You dash into your house. In your room, you switch on your computer and slip the floppy into the drive.

Your eyes widen. "Awesome! Totally, completely, amazingly awesome!" You can't take your eyes off the screen.

All the next year's computer games are on this disk. You scroll through the files. Every major company!

You can play them all before anyone else!

You click open a file. Whoa — neat! *Nuclear Ninja* added sound effects! You open another. *Destroyer* added four new levels! This is fantastic. You could sit here for hours!

BANG! CRASH! WHAM!

You're so startled you fall off your desk chair. When you glance up, you discover a thug in an overcoat and sunglasses standing in your doorway. Your *broken-down* doorway. And there's another leaning in your window. Your *smashed* window.

Uh-oh. Guess what?

It's GAME OVER for you!

THE END

124

Suddenly, your flashlights blink out.

"Oh, no!" you gasp. "What's wrong with the flashlights?"

"Look at the sky!" Sophie yells.

You glance up. Your mouth drops open in awe.

The sky is lit up with shooting stars. Hundreds of specks of light dance in the blackness. The night becomes almost as bright as day.

"There must be hundreds of them," Andrew murmurs.

You gaze at the dazzling sight. "It's beautiful," you say. Then you glance over at the rose garden. You begin to tremble.

The eggs are completely visible in the brilliant light of the meteor shower. They bounce around on the ground. You hear a low rumbling sound, like a refrigerator humming.

It's coming from the eggs.

"I think they're about to hatch!" you shout.

Turn to PAGE 131.

To quote Andrew, "Are you nuts?"

You must not read these books very often.

Otherwise you would know better.

Do you actually think that Grandma will tell you why she has boxes of hands and feet? Why she has a mask that could pass for your mom? What the deal is with the rose garden and the meteors?

Okay, maybe she *will* tell you.

But *then* what will she do?

Chances are, it won't be pretty.

Very, very quickly and very, very quietly turn back to PAGE 127. And make a different choice.

"You're probably right," Sophie says. "We should destroy the eggs."

"Yeah," Andrew agrees. "Better safe than sorry, I guess."

"Do you think stepping on them will work?" Sophie asks. "They look awfully big and sturdy."

"One way to find out," you tell her. You stride toward one of the eggs. You lift up your foot and bring it down hard.

KA-BOOM!!!!!!!!!

Whoops.

Guess you didn't notice the little purple land mines mixed in with the purple alien eggs. Grandma placed them in the garden to protect her babies.

Oh, well. Better luck next mine. . . .

THE END

All clear!

Sophie pulls out one of the shoe boxes from the closet. "She's got other stuff in here too," she informs you. She holds up a wig. Andrew reaches in and pulls out a mask.

It looks exactly like your mother!

You feel your own very real face go pale. "Why would Grandma have something like that?" you ask.

"Hey, look at this!" Sophie holds up a pile of newspaper clippings. "They're all about the meteor shower tonight."

"I don't get it!" you wail. "None of this makes any sense. Why would Grandma have these things? Why is she obsessed with the rose garden? And those clippings! What is *up* with all this?"

"I think you should go ask her," Sophie suggests.

"Are you nuts?" Andrew scoffs. "We should wait until the meteor shower and see if she does something."

Follow Sophie's advice and ask Grandma "What's up?" on PAGE 125.

Wait and see what happens during the meteor shower on PAGE 5.

"Quick!" you shriek. "Lift!"

You, Chuck, and Ginny hoist the heavy mirror over your heads. It pierces the orange beam. The rays bend and bounce off the mirror—straight at the two thugs.

The two creatures stand frozen in place.

"It's working!" you cry. "Grab Grandma!"

You lean the mirror against a luggage rack, aiming the beam directly at the creatures. Chuck and Ginny lift Grandma out of the chair. She's still out cold, but at least you've rescued her from the force field.

"Out the back!" you shout. "Hurry!"

Chuck and Ginny drag Grandma out the back door. You follow right behind them.

Oops. You forgot you were in the last car.

"So, genius," Ginny says as she strains to hold up Grandma. "Now what?"

Turn to PAGE 96.

"Do you know what EMPLEH means?" you ask Grandma.

"Empleh?" she repeats. "No, I've never heard that word before. Why do you ask?"

"I saw it written on that train window." You turn and point back to the train car. "I think it's some kind of message."

Grandma grabs your hand and links her arm through yours. "My, my," she coos. "You have such an imagination."

Is Grandma walking faster? Or is that your imagination too?

"It's wonderful to see you after so long," she gushes, hurrying down the platform. "And I can't wait to see your mother's lovely rose garden."

"Yeah, right," you murmur. You're still trying to figure out what EMPLEH means.

You snap your fingers. "I know what it means!" you cry.

Turn to PAGE 31.

130

You gaze down at the garden. You wonder how long it will be before the aliens come after you.

Then you notice something strange. The creatures slither easily out from under the objects you've thrown down on them. But the aliens near the radio shrivel up and fall over!

"The radio!" you shout. "It destroys them! They must be allergic to sound waves, or something."

"Awesome!" Andrew yells. "We found a weapon!"

You dash into your room and get your radio. Sophie grabs your cassette player and pops in a tape. Andrew snatches the portable CD player. You race downstairs and into the garden.

You aim the radio at a group of creatures. Their slimy skin puckers, turning black. They curl up. Little wisps of smoke rise from their crinkly bodies.

It's working!

Sophie and Andrew use the tape and CD players in the same way. Little aliens are shriveling all around you.

"*Nooo!*" a voice bellows.

Grandma!

Turn to PAGE 112.

"Get ready!" you holler.

Sophie and Andrew clutch their water guns. You aim yours directly at the pulsing, humming egg in front of you.

The night sky brightens even more. With a roar, the eggs burst open! Bits of purple eggshell rain down on you. Creatures crawl out of the eggs. Each one of them is different!

A striped, football-shaped creature scuttles up to you on twelve spidery legs. Your finger tightens on the trigger of your water gun.

Go to PAGE 32.

About R.L. Stine

R.L. STINE is the most popular author in America. He is the creator of the *Goosebumps*, *Give Yourself Goosebumps*, *Fear Street*, and *Ghosts of Fear Street* series, among other popular books. He has written more than 100 scary novels for kids. Bob lives in New York City with his wife, Jane, teenage son, Matt, and dog, Nadine.